CARTER HIGH™
CHRONICLES

BACK-UP
Quarterback

By Eleanor Robins

SADDLEBACK™
EDUCATIONAL PUBLISHING

CARTER HIGH™
C H R O N I C L E S

SADDLEBACK™
EDUCATIONAL PUBLISHING
www.sdlback.com

ISBN-13: 978-1-61651-303-0
ISBN-10: 1-61651-303-9
eBook: 978-1-60291-951-8

Printed in Guangzhou, China
0911/CA21101491

15 14 13 12 11   2 3 4 5 6

Chapter 1

Dan was in his front yard. Kirk was there too. Kirk was his best friend.

"What do you want to do?" Dan asked.

"I don't know. What do you want to do?" Kirk asked.

Dan said, "Practice starts next week. I could throw some passes to you."

"OK," Kirk said.

Dan was on the football team. Kirk was on the tennis team. But Kirk also helped the football team.

Dan got his football from the house. Then both boys went to Dan's backyard.

Kirk said, "What are you and Eve

going to do this weekend?"

Eve was Dan's girlfriend. They had been dating for almost a year.

Dan said, "We're going to a show. What are you and Claire going to do?"

Claire was Kirk's girlfriend. They had been dating for about two months.

Kirk said, "Claire has to go out of town. She has to go see her grandmother one weekend each month."

The boys threw the ball to each other for a while.

Then Dan said, "What do you think?"

"About what?" Kirk asked.

"Will I be the quarterback this year?" Dan said.

The team would need a new quarterback.

Dan hoped he would be the quarterback. Last year he had been the back-up quarterback.

Two other boys were going to try out for the job. He and Kirk knew them.

Kirk said, "You should be. You pass better than the other guys. So the coach should pick you."

Dan was sure he would be the quarterback too. He could hardly wait for the season to start.

The boys threw some more passes to each other.

Then Dan said, "Know any news?"

Not much had been going on all week.

"One thing," Kirk said.

"What?" Dan asked.

"A new guy moved in down the street from me. But I haven't met him yet," Kirk said.

"Know anything about him?" Dan asked.

Kirk said, "Yeah. He played on the football team at his other school."

"What did he play?" Dan asked.

Kirk said, "I heard he's a running back. But I don't know for sure."

They could use a new running back on the team.

Dan said, "I hope he is a back. We sure could use one more good back."

Kirk said, "I'll let you know as soon as I find out. I'm going to try to meet him before practice starts."

Dan heard the phone ring.

Dan said, "I hear the phone. I'll be back in a few minutes."

Dan hurried into the house. Kirk stayed out in the yard.

The phone call was for Dan.

It was Coach Grant.

Dan got very excited.

Did Coach Grant call to tell him he would be the quarterback?

Chapter 2

Coach Grant said, "I'm at school, Dan. I need to talk to you. Do you have time to come over here?"

"Sure. When?" Dan asked.

"As soon as you can," Coach Grant said.

Dan said, "Kirk is here. Do you want him to come too?"

"No. Just you, Dan," Coach Grant said.

"I'll be right over," Dan said.

Dan hurried outside.

"Who was it?" Kirk asked.

Dan said, "Coach Grant. He wants me at school. He wants to talk to me."

"Does he want to talk to me too?" Kirk asked.

Dan said, "No. I asked him. He just wants to see me."

"Why do you think he wants to see you?" Kirk asked.

"Maybe to tell me I will be the quarterback. And to go over some plays with me," Dan said.

"Good luck. I will be at home. Let me know what he wanted," Kirk said.

Dan said, "Thanks. I'll stop by your house on the way home. And I will tell you all about it."

Dan hurried to the school.

Coach Grant was in his office. His office door was open. He was sitting at his desk. He was looking at some papers on his desk.

Dan knocked on the door.

The coach looked up. He said,

"Thanks for coming, Dan. Come in and shut the door."

Why did the coach want him to shut the door? That didn't sound good to Dan.

"Sit down, Dan," Coach Grant said.

Why did the coach ask him to sit down? Did he have bad news for Dan? Or was he just going to go over some plays with Dan?

Coach Grant said, "A new guy is going out for the team. He is from out of state. His name is Clay. He is going to try out for quarterback."

Coach Grant quit talking. He seemed to be waiting for Dan to say something.

But Dan was too surprised to know what to say.

"I wanted you to hear that from me, Dan. And not from someone else," Coach Grant said.

Dan made himself say, "Thanks for telling me."

Coach Grant said, "Clay gave me a letter from his coach. Last year Clay was one of the top players in his state."

What was the coach trying to tell Dan? Was it that Clay would be the quarterback? And not him?

Dan had to know. He said, "What are you telling me? That he will be the quarterback this year?"

Slowly Coach Grant said, "Maybe, Dan. I won't know until I see both of you at practice. The better player will get the job. I hope it is you. You worked hard last year. But you need to know it might be Clay."

Dan didn't want to stay there any longer. He had to get out of there.

Dan said, "OK for me to go? Or did you need to see me about something else?"

"No. That's all, Dan. You can go," Coach Grant said.

Dan got out of there as fast as he could. He was very upset.

He had worked so hard to be the quarterback. It was not fair that a new kid might get the job.

Chapter 3

Dan walked as fast as he could away from the school. He almost ran.

Soon he got to Kirk's house. Kirk was in his front yard. He was waiting for Dan.

Kirk said, "What's wrong? I can see from your face that you are upset. Why did Coach Grant want to see you?"

"To tell me I might not be the quarter-back. That a new guy might be," Dan said.

Kirk looked very surprised. He said, "Who?"

"Some kid from out of state. His

name is Clay," Dan said.

"He must be the one who moved in down the street. I heard he is from out of state," Kirk said.

For a few minutes the boys didn't talk.

Then Dan said, "I worked hard last year. And in spring practice."

"I know you did," Kirk said.

"I should be the one to have that job. Not some new kid," Dan said.

"I think you should have it too," Kirk said.

For a few more minutes the boys didn't talk.

Then Dan said, "It isn't fair. I tried to learn as much as I could last year. I should be the quarterback this year."

"Yeah. You should be," Kirk said.

"I didn't work that hard to be back-up quarterback again. And to sit on the bench most of the time," Dan said.

Kirk said, "Maybe you won't be the backup. Maybe the new kid is not that good."

Dan said, "Coach Grant has a letter from his coach. He was one of the best players in his state."

Kirk looked surprised.

For a few more minutes the boys didn't talk.

Then Dan said, "I might not go out for the team this year."

"Why?" Kirk asked. He looked even more surprised.

Dan said, "It is too much work. Just to be the back-up. And sit on the bench."

"Did the coach say Clay would be the quarterback for sure? Or just that he might be?" Kirk asked.

"Just that he might be," Dan said.

Kirk said, "Then don't give up now. You have to try out. You have worked too hard to give up now."

Dan knew Kirk was right. He should try out. But Dan didn't think it would do any good to try.

Dan knew Clay would get the job.

Chapter 4

It was the first day of practice. Dan was on his way to Kirk's house. He was glad Kirk helped with the team.

Dan walked slowly. He was in no hurry to get to practice. He was sure Clay would be the new quarterback.

Kirk was in his yard. He was waiting for Dan.

Kirk said, "I'm glad you are still going out for the team."

But Dan wasn't sure he was glad. It wouldn't be any fun to lose his job to a new boy. Dan knew it really wasn't his job. But he felt like it was.

Soon Dan and Kirk got to school. They saw some guys they didn't know. One of them must be Clay.

They also saw a lot of guys they knew. One of them was Griff. Griff had been in some of their classes last year.

Kirk said, "I sure am surprised to see Griff here. Football is hard work. And Griff doesn't like hard work."

Dan said, "I'm surprised to see him too."

Dan and Kirk talked to some of the boys they knew.

Then Coach Grant said, "Time to start. This week we will spend a lot of time going over plays. And getting you in shape to play. But first I want you to meet the new guys."

Dan was glad. He wanted to know who Clay was.

A new kid was standing next to Coach

Grant. The coach looked at him.

Then the coach said, "This is Clay. He just moved here from out of state. He was one of the best players in his state last year."

Most of the boys yelled loudly. But Dan and Kirk didn't.

"What does he play?" Griff asked.

"Quarterback," the coach said.

All the players from last year looked at Dan. They knew Clay would be after Dan's job. But Dan tried to look like he didn't care.

They knew it wasn't his job. But all the boys had thought it would be.

Coach Grant told them who the other new kids were. Then he said, "All of you help these guys out. Make them feel welcome."

The coach said that to all of them. But Dan felt like the coach said it just to him.

"You can talk to the new players for a few minutes. Then we will get to work. We have a lot to do this week," Coach Grant said.

Dan looked at Clay. Clay was looking at him.

Clay walked over to Dan.

Clay said, "I saw the guys look at you. You must be the guy the coach told me about. The one who was the back-up quarterback last year."

"Yeah. I am," Dan said.

Clay said, "Then I should tell you. I plan to try out for quarterback. I just wanted you to know. I hope there will be no hard feelings."

Dan made himself say, "No. May the best player win."

Clay was new to the team. Why did he have to try out for quarterback?

Didn't he care that Dan had worked hard for the job?

It wasn't fair he might be the quarterback and not Dan.

Chapter 5

Dan worked very hard the first week of practice. But so did Clay.

It was the second week of practice. They were doing exercises. The guys who helped the team were doing them too.

Griff was next to Dan. He said, "The coach sure is working us hard."

Dan said, "He has to. We have to be in shape for the first game."

"This is no fun. I might quit," Griff said.

Dan and Kirk looked at each other. They tried not to laugh. They weren't surprised Griff said that. They knew

Griff didn't like to work hard.

"How long do you give him?" Kirk asked Dan. But he said it so Griff couldn't hear him.

"About one more week," Dan said.

Kirk laughed.

Coach Grant said, "Stop for a few minutes, boys. The exercises can wait. I need to talk with all of you."

All the players stopped. They looked at Coach Grant.

The coach did not look pleased. Dan wondered what he was going to say to them.

Coach Grant said, "Some of you guys are giving Clay a hard time."

Dan wasn't. And Kirk wasn't. But Dan knew some of his friends were. Clay was trying out for quarterback. And they didn't like it. They wanted Dan to be the quarterback.

Coach Grant said, "Clay can't help it that he is new here. He wants to be on his old team. But he can't be. He is here now. So treat him like you would want to be treated."

Dan looked at Clay. Clay looked like he wished the coach had not said anything.

Coach Grant said, "Clay didn't tell me about this. But I can see what is going on. And I don't want to see that again. Now back to work."

They started doing their exercises. None of them was talking.

Coach Grant walked off from the boys. He was standing by himself. He said, "Come over here, Dan. I need to talk to you."

Dan wondered why. Did he think Dan had given Clay a hard time?

Dan ran over to the coach. He knew

all the guys were looking at him. And wondering why the coach wanted to talk to him.

Coach Grant said, "I need your help, Dan."

Dan was too surprised to say anything.

Why did the coach need his help?

Coach Grant said, "Clay doesn't know all of our plays. And how we do things here. I know it is a lot to ask of you. But I want you to help Clay as much as you can. Can you work with him one day after practice?"

Dan couldn't believe he heard the coach right.

"You want me to help Clay?" he asked.

How could Coach Grant ask him to help Clay?

Dan didn't think he could do that. It wasn't fair.

Coach Grant said, "Yes, Dan. I know I am asking a lot of you. But you have always done your best for the team. And I am counting on you to do that now."

How could Dan help Clay? He would be helping Clay to take the job he wanted. The job he should have.

"Can I count on you to help Clay?" Coach Grant asked.

Dan didn't answer.

"Do it for the team, Dan," Coach Grant said.

How could Dan say no? He might not get to be the quarterback. But he cared about the team. He had played with most of the guys last year.

"OK," Dan said.

The coach said, "Thanks, Dan. I knew I could count on you."

Dan knew he was doing the right

thing. But he didn't feel good about it.

"When do you want me to help him? Today?" Dan asked.

"That's up to you, Dan. But as soon as you can," Coach Grant said.

"I'll ask him about meeting today after practice," Dan said.

Coach Grant said, "Thanks, Dan. Do you want me to call Clay over? So you can ask him now?"

"OK," Dan said. But he didn't want to help Clay. Or even talk to him.

"Clay, come over here. We need you," Coach Grant said.

Clay hurried over to them.

All the guys were looking at them.

Coach Grant said, "Dan said he would help you learn some plays. You can set up a time to get together."

The coach walked away.

At first the two boys just looked at each other.

Then Dan said, "My house OK? After practice today?"

"Sure. Where do you live?" Clay asked.

Dan told him. Then Dan said, "You can walk home with me. Or you can meet me there."

Clay said, "I'll meet you there. I told my mom I would be home right after practice. So I need to go by my house. And tell my mom where I will be."

"OK. See you later at my house," Dan said.

Then Dan walked over to Kirk.

"What did Coach Grant want?" Kirk asked.

Dan said, "For me to help Clay. One day after practice."

"Why?" Kirk asked.

"Clay doesn't know a lot of our plays," Dan said.

"Did you say you would help him?" Kirk asked.

Dan said, "Yeah. But I don't want to help him. I told Clay I would help him today. At my house. And I want you there with us."

"OK," Kirk said.

All the boys got back to work.

Dan worked hard. But practice ended too quickly for him. He was in no hurry to help Clay.

Dan and Kirk walked to Dan's house. It wasn't long before Clay got there.

Dan and Kirk went over some plays with Clay. Clay told them about some plays at his old school.

Then it was time for Clay to go.

Clay said, "Thanks for the help. It means a lot that you would help me."

Clay was looking at Dan when he said that.

"Any time," Dan made himself say.

"See you at practice tomorrow," Clay said. Then he left.

Kirk said, "He seems OK. Too bad he wants to be the quarterback."

Dan thought he seemed OK too. Dan might have liked him.

But it wasn't fair Clay might be the quarterback. And not Dan.

Chapter 6

It was only a few days until the first game.

Dan was at practice. It was the first day they would have two teams. And keep score.

Dan had worked very hard at all the practices. But so had Clay. And Dan had helped Clay at some of the practices.

The boys did some exercises. Then Coach Grant said, "Time to play a game."

Dan hoped he would play on Team 1. Team 1 players almost always started the first game.

"Good luck," Kirk said to Dan. But he

said it so only Dan could hear him.

"Team 1," Coach Grant said. He started to call out the names.

Who would the quarterback be? Dan could hardly wait for the coach to say. Dan thought he should be. But the coach might think Clay should be.

Coach Grant said, "Clay, you be the quarterback."

Dan tried to look like he didn't care. He didn't want the other guys to see how upset he was.

Then Coach Grant said, "Dan, tomorrow you will be the quarterback."

That made Dan feel better. But not a lot better.

Clay's team got the ball first. The team did not score. But the team did make three first downs.

"Good job, Clay," Coach said.

"Thanks, Coach," Clay said.

It was Dan's turn to play quarterback on Team 2.

On the first two plays Dan handed the ball off. The first guy made three yards. But the second guy got stopped behind the line.

Then Dan threw a pass. But he threw it too far. A player on Team 1 almost got it.

Dan's team had to kick.

A player on his team said, "Don't worry, Dan. We'll do better next time."

"Sure we will," another player said.

But things didn't get any better.

Dan got pulled down behind the line two times. Most of his long passes were not good. And Team 1 got three of his passes.

His team scored only one touchdown. Clay's team scored four. His long passes were good. But he got mixed-up on some of the plays.

After practice Kirk said, "Don't worry,

Dan. You will be on Team 1 tomorrow with the good players. And you will do better."

"Sure I will," Dan said. But he really wasn't sure he would.

Did the team do badly? Or was Clay the better quarterback?

The next day Dan was the Team 1 quarterback. The team scored two touchdowns. But he was pulled down behind the line one time. Most of his long passes were not good. And Team 2 almost got two of his passes.

Clay's team scored two touchdowns too. But Clay still got mixed-up on some of the plays.

Dan was glad when the game was over.

"How did I do?" he asked Kirk.

"The game was a tie. So you did OK," Kirk said.

But they both knew Dan's team should have won.

The next day Dan and Clay took turns being the Team 1 quarterback. And three players took turns being running backs. One of them was very good. The other two were trying out for the job. But they did not play well.

The next day Coach Grant called Dan over to the side. He said, "Clay still hasn't learned all of our plays. And you know the other players better than he does. So I am going to put you in as a running back. You can help Clay when he needs it."

Just great, Dan thought. Clay wasn't doing well. And now Dan had to help him get Dan's job.

"That OK with you?" Coach Grant asked.

"Sure," Dan said. But he didn't really mean it.

Dan walked over to Kirk.

"What did the coach say?" Kirk asked.

"He is putting me in as a running back," Dan said.

Kirk said, "Good. We need a running back."

Dan said, "That isn't why. He said Clay hasn't learned all of our plays. And he wants me to help Clay."

Dan played running back. And he helped Clay when Clay needed help. And he was the quarterback for Team 2.

Dan worked very hard. But so did Clay. They both played well. But they both needed to do better on some things.

Who was the better player?

And who would Coach Grant pick to be the quarterback?

Chapter 7

Dan was walking home from practice. Kirk was with him.

Dan could hardly wait for the next day to come. Coach Grant would name the starting team.

"What do you think?" Dan asked.

"About what?" Kirk asked.

"Who should be the quarterback? Clay or me?" Dan asked.

"You," Kirk said.

Dan said, "Do you really think that? Or did you just say that because you are my best friend?"

Kirk didn't answer right away. But

then he said, "I really think that."

But Kirk didn't look at Dan when he said it.

Dan said, "We have never lied to each other, Kirk. So don't lie to me now. Who is better? Clay or me?"

Kirk didn't answer right away. And he didn't look at Dan when he did.

"Well, Clay is good," Kirk said.

"So you think Coach Grant should pick him," Dan said.

Kirk said, "I didn't say that."

"You didn't have to," Dan said.

His best friend thought Clay should be the quarterback. So how could Dan hope the coach would pick him?

That night Coach Grant called Dan.

The coach said, "I need to see you, Dan. Can you come by my office before school tomorrow?"

"Sure," Dan said.

"I will see you then," the coach said.

Dan knew why Coach Grant wanted to see him. It was to tell him who the quarterback would be. But Dan already knew.

It would be Clay.

It would not be Dan. Or the coach would have told him on the phone.

Dan called Kirk.

Dan said, "Coach Grant just called. He wants to see me tomorrow before school."

"Did he say why?" Kirk asked.

Dan said, "No. But I know why. He wants to tell me he picked Clay."

"Maybe not," Kirk said.

But Dan was sure Kirk thought that too.

Kirk said, "Want me to go with you? And wait outside the office?"

"Yeah," Dan said.

Dan would want to talk to Kirk after he saw the coach. They always shared good and bad news with each other.

The next morning Kirk walked to school with Dan. And he walked to the coach's office with Dan. The door was open.

Kirk said, "Good luck, Dan. Maybe it is not what you think." Kirk said it so only Dan could hear him.

Coach Grant was at his desk. He saw Dan.

The coach said, "Come in, Dan. Close the door. And sit down."

Dan went in and closed the door. He sat down.

Coach Grant said, "I wanted to talk to you before practice. You may have guessed why."

Dan didn't say anything.

Coach Grant said, "This is very hard

for me, Dan. You have worked very hard. I really wanted you to be the quarterback."

Dan knew what the coach would say next.

The coach said, "I'm sorry, Dan. But I had to pick the better player. Clay can throw better than you. And he can scramble better than you."

Dan knew the coach was right. But he knew the plays better. And he knew his teammates better than Clay did.

Coach Grant said, "I plan to tell the team at practice today. And I wanted you to know before then."

Dan was glad the coach told him before school. And not at practice.

Coach Grant said, "A team needs a good quarterback. But a good team needs more than that."

The team needed a good back-up

quarterback too. Dan was sure that was what the coach would say. He didn't want to hear that.

Dan stood up. He had to get out of there.

Dan said, "OK for me to go? I have to see a teacher before school starts. And I can't be late."

But he did not have to see a teacher.

Coach Grant said, "Sure, Dan. You can go. I will talk to you at practice."

Dan hurried out of the office. Kirk was waiting for him.

Kirk said, "Don't tell me. I can read your face. Anything I can do?"

"No," Dan said.

Nothing could make him feel better.

He had helped Clay to get the job. It was not fair.

Dan wanted to quit the team. He should have quit when Griff did. But it was too late to quit now. He knew what the other boys would think. They would know he quit because of Clay.

He had to try to make the best of it.

But it would not be easy.

Chapter 8

Dan did not want to go to practice that afternoon. But he had to go. Kirk was walking to the field with him.

"Who do you think will be the other running back? Both of the guys play about the same. And that is not so good," Kirk said.

"I don't know," Dan said.

Dan didn't care who the other running back was. All he cared about was who the quarterback was.

Kirk said, "You played as well as they did. Maybe better."

They got to the field. They saw Clay.

He looked very happy.

Clay came over to them. He said, "The coach said he told you. Thanks for the help. I couldn't have gotten the job without your help."

Coach Grant called to Dan before he could say anything. The coach said, "Come over here, Dan. I need to talk to you."

Dan started to walk over to Coach Grant. He didn't run. He didn't want to hear about the back-up quarterback job. About how every good team needed a good back-up quarterback.

Coach Grant said, "I wanted to ask you something this morning. But you had to go before I could, Dan."

"What?" Dan asked. Did he want to ask Dan to keep helping Clay?

"You worked hard this year and last year. You have been a good team player.

And you have helped Clay. You should be on the starting team," Coach Grant said.

Dan thought so too. But what was the coach trying to say?

Coach Grant said, "We need a running back. No one has earned the job. Would you like to give it a try?"

Dan was very surprised.

"I know that is not the same as being quarterback. But you would be on the first team. And you could still be the back-up quarterback. It might not work out. But give it a try," Coach Grant said.

Dan didn't know what to say.

Coach Grant said, "You are a team player, Dan. You put the needs of the team before your needs. You should have a try at being on the starting team."

Dan was still too surprised to know what to say.

"What do you say, Dan? Will you give

it a try?" Coach Grant asked.

The other two players wanted the job. But they had not earned it. So he wouldn't be taking their job away from them. It would be OK for him to give it a try.

"Sure. Why not," Dan said.

It would not be the same as being the starting quarterback. But Dan would get to be on the starting team. Maybe it would not work out. But he would give it a try. And he would try to do his best.

Mystery at MANZANAR

A WWII INTERNMENT CAMP STORY

by Eric Fein

illustrated by
Kurt Hartman

Librarian Reviewer
Laurie K. Holland
Media Specialist (National Board Certified), Edina, MN
MA in Elementary Education, Minnesota State University, Mankato

Reading Consultant
Elizabeth Stedem
Educator/Consultant, Colorado Springs, CO
MA in Elementary Education, University of Denver, CO

STONE ARCH BOOKS
www.stonearchbooks.com

Graphic Flash is published by Stone Arch Books
1710 Roe Crest Drive
North Mankato, Minnesota 56003
www.stonearchbooks.com

Library of Congress Cataloging-in-Publication Data
Fein, Eric.
    Mystery at Manzanar: A WWII Internment Camp Story / by Eric Fein;
illustrated by Kurt Hartman.
    p. cm. — (Graphic Flash)
    ISBN 978-1-4342-0751-7 (library binding : alk. paper)
    ISBN 978-1-4342-0847-7 (pbk. : alk. paper)
    1. Graphic novels. [1. Graphic novels. 2. Japanese Americans—Evacuation and
relocation, 1942–1945—Fiction. 3. Manzanar War Relocation Center—Fiction.
4. Mystery and detective stories.] I. Hartman, Kurt, ill. II. Title.
PZ7.7.F45My 2009
[Fic]—dc22   2008006669

Summary: During World War II, 15-year-old Tommy Yamamoto and his family are
forced into the Manzanar interment camp for Japanese Americans. While there, an
elderly internee is attacked, and one of the camp's guards is charged with the crime.
Tommy sets out to solve the crime and discovers some unlikely suspects.

Art Director: Heather Kindseth
Graphic Designer: Brann Garvey

Printed in the United States of America in North Mankato, Minnesota.
072016 010671R

Table of Contents

Introducing . . .

Tommy Yamamoto

Joey Okada

Mr. Hiro Sakata

4

PRIVATE DWAYNE COLLINS

PRIVATE JOHN O'MALLEY

VICTOR KUDO

5

CHAPTER 1

Taken Captive

They came as we were having dinner. They didn't bother to knock. Ever since the attack on Pearl Harbor, the United States government didn't trust Japanese Americans. Now, they were going to take us away.

My parents came to America in 1915. They had little money but managed to buy a small farm. They wanted to raise a family and live as Americans. However, because my parents are *Issei*, meaning they were born in Japan, they are not allowed to become American citizens. My sister, Mary, and I are *Nisei*. We were born here in California. We are legal citizens of the United States. Sadly, most Americans view us as outsiders. They see danger in our faces.

"What right do you have to break into my home?" my father yelled.

"I'm Agent Fisk. The War Department ordered us to search this house," the man replied.

For the next three hours, the agents tore apart our home. A couple of them seemed to enjoy making a mess of our things. In the end, they found nothing. I don't know what they expected to find. My parents were farmers, not spies.

"Good work, men," Agent Fisk said. "Take Mr. Yamamoto to the office so we can question him some more."

"No! My husband has done nothing wrong," Mother shouted.

"I have my orders," said Agent Fisk. "All Japanese on the West Coast of the United States are being moved inland for national security."

As the agents grabbed my father's arm, my mother started to cry. My father looked at her with a sad smile. "Easy, Tamiko," he said. "I'll be fine."

The next two weeks were a blur. We were told that we were being moved for our own good. We weren't told where we were going. We could only take what we could carry. Everything else was sold or put in storage with neighbors.

Besides my clothes, the only thing I packed was a book. It was a collection of Sherlock Holmes mystery stories. I loved reading them. Sherlock Holmes always based his conclusions on cold hard facts. That was something the rest of the world seemed unable to do at the moment.

Our family first went to an assembly center. This was a place used to house thousands of Japanese Americans being removed from their homes. Our assembly center was a racetrack. We had to live in a stall where horses had been kept. It was cramped and smelly. After a month, we were sent to a camp that would be our new home.

It was a long, hot train ride to the camp. Each time the train went through a town, the people there yelled hateful things at us.

CHAPTER 2

Days later, we arrived at the camp, the
Manzanar Relocation Center. It was in the
California desert, miles from any town. A fence
topped with barbed wire surrounded the area.

There were two guard towers at the front and
back of the camp. Guards with machine guns
stood in the towers watching over us. The first
time I saw them, it gave me an ice-cold knot in
the pit of my stomach. It wasn't just the guns that
made them scary. It was the angry look on their
faces.

Despite the armed guards, our families settled
into a daily routine at Manzanar. Adults got jobs
in the camp. Children went to school.

The camp was divided into blocks. Each block was made up of 14 buildings called barracks.

Each block had its own mess hall. You had to wait in line be served food.

Some people worked together to grow fresh fruit and vegetables for the camp.

Sometimes after school we would play catch near the front gate. This way we could see who was visiting the camp or leaving it. It gave us a small reminder that there was life outside the barbed wire.

16

Some of the guards were nice. Others were nasty. Dwayne Collins was one of the nasty ones. Victor Kudo, one of the older boys at school, hated them all. He was always looking for a fight. When that happened, my friend Joey and I didn't stick around.

Sometimes, Victor got in fights at school when he called another boy an *inu*. I knew that *inu* was the Japanese word for dog. I didn't understand why that made people so angry.

"An *inu* is an informer," Joey explained to me one day. "It's someone who works on the side of the guards. Not on our side."

"I thought we were all on the same side," I said. "Aren't we all Americans?"

CHAPTER 3

The Crime

One morning, Joey and I stopped to chat with our neighbor, Mr. Sakata. Mr. Sakata was sitting in front of his barracks carving something out of a piece of wood. Since coming to the camp, he had carved about fifteen figurines. He kept them proudly displayed on a tiny shelf above his bed.

"What are you carving today?" Joey asked.

"A bald eagle," Mr. Sakata said. "It's the symbol of our country." Even though the government had sent him here to Manzanar, he could not find it in his heart to hate America.

"Wow, that's swell," Joey said. "Can I hold it?"

Mr. Sakata smiled. "Maybe when it's finished."

After school, I went right back to my family's quarters and stayed in my bed, reading.

"Tommy, it is time for dinner," Mother said.

"I'm not hungry," I said.

She sat on the edge of my bed and placed her hand on my forehead. "Do you have a fever?"

"No," I said.

She saw I was reading my Sherlock Holmes book again. "You read too many mysteries," she said. "They have too much violence. They make you upset. That's why you have no appetite."

"No, mom," I said. "I'm just not hungry."

"After dinner, do you want to go to a movie at the mess hall?" she asked.

"Nah. I just don't feel like it today," I said.

"Okay," she said. "I'll let you have your way this time."

I had seen the notice earlier in the day saying that a Roy Rogers western was going to be shown. Usually, I liked cowboy movies. But after running into Collins twice, I didn't want to risk a third.

Through the open window, I could hear Mr. Sakata hum as he put the finishing touches on his carving. I kept reading my Sherlock Holmes book.

Reading let me forget my troubles. After a few pages, I wasn't in an internment camp. Instead, I was with Sherlock Holmes chasing criminals through the foggy streets of London.

But then . . .

What was that?

Mr. Sakata!

CHAPTER 4

Under Suspicion

I was taken before the camp's head security officer. Representatives from my barracks' block joined him. I was scared. I really wished my father could be here with me. But we still didn't know where he was or if we would ever hear from him again. I reminded myself that I was the man of the family, and I would have to fix this situation myself.

Collins and John were standing on either side of me. Collins had just finished telling his version of events. Of course, he eagerly painted me as the attacker.

"How is Mr. Sakata doing?" asked the security officer.

"We took him over to the infirmary," John said. "Doc says he got a few bruises. He's going to keep him overnight for observation. Sakata should be okay in a day or two."

The security officer nodded, then looked at me.

Son, a man that old could have died.

I would never hurt Mr. Sakata.

I saw you right next to him, kid.

If I did attack him, then what did I do with his carving?

"You could have thrown it into the bushes or hidden it somewhere nearby," Collins said.

"Sir, I really don't think Tommy did this," said John. "I've seen him with Mr. Sakata several times, and they get along pretty well."

"I want a search team set up to see if this carving can be found," the security officer said. "In the meantime, Private O'Malley, I want you to take this young man back to his barracks. He will stay there until we can figure this out."

The security officer looked me straight in the eye and said, "If you cause any more trouble, son, you'll leave me no choice but to have you locked up. Understand?"

"Yes, sir," I said quietly. John took me by the arm and led me outside. As the door closed behind us, he let go.

"Thanks for standing up for me," I said.

When I got home, my mother was waiting. She was very upset. News of what happened to Mr. Sakata had spread like wildfire throughout the camp. She was afraid that I would be sent away.

Later that night, we were woken up by a loud knock at the door. *Were the guards coming back for me?* I wondered.

"Victor! What are you doing here?" my mother exclaimed as she opened the door.

"I have to talk to Tommy about what happened last night," he said.

"My son is innocent!" Mother shouted. "He would never hurt another person!"

"I know," Victor said, turning toward me. "It was John O'Malley, the camp guard."

"Huh?" I couldn't believe my ears. "It couldn't have been John. He treats us better than any of the guards."

"They found Mr. Sakata's carving in his locker," Victor said. "It was just another trick to keep us in line."

"What will happen to John?" I asked.

"He'll probably be sent to jail," he replied. "For now, he's been confined to his quarters."

"I have to speak to the security officer," I said.

"Why?" Victor asked, puzzled.

CHAPTER 5

Tommy Investigates

Early the next morning, I caught up with the head security officer as he was walking toward his office. "Son, you are giving me a headache," he said. "This case is closed."

"I'm sorry, sir," I said. "But I know that John O'Malley couldn't have attacked Mr. Sakata."

"You have any proof?" he asked.

"No, sir," I replied. "I just know that he didn't do it. What reason would he have to hurt Mr. Sakata?"

"I don't know," the officer said, turning to walk away. "But I can't have a guard in this camp that everyone thinks is dangerous. We've already had one riot here. I don't want another."

31

"It happened so quickly. I never saw who it was," Mr. Sakata continued. "My wife told me that one of the guards did it."

"Yes, John O'Malley," I said. "But I think that they got the wrong person."

"What are you saying?" Mr. Sakata asked.

"I know that John would never do something so terrible," I replied. "He is a good man."

"A good man does not attack people and take their belongings," he said.

"But there's no proof. And it just doesn't make any sense," I said. "Besides, it's only a rumor."

"I will not speak about this anymore," he said, pointing toward the door.

"I'm sorry, Mr. Sakata," I said.

Next, I went to find Collins. He was on duty at the front gate.

"I thought John was your friend," I asked.

"Nah, he's just someone to talk to," Collins replied. "Who else am I going to talk to in this dustbowl? You?

"Last time I saw John, he was in the mess hall having dinner. I left him there to go on duty. That was a good hour before the attack."

I left feeling totally discouraged. Then, as I headed for dinner, Victor and his two friends spotted me. "Hey!" Victor yelled. "Are you trying to help clear the guard?"

Dusting myself off, I realized that I hadn't gotten any closer to solving the case. No one seemed to have any answers. Now Victor and his friends weren't going to make this case any easier. I needed to hear John's side of the story. Maybe he could help rule out some of the suspects.

On the way to the officers' barracks, I ran into Joey. He was wearing his mitt and his baseball cleats. I had been so busy, I completely forgot about the baseball game.

"How'd the game go?" I asked.

"We could have used you," he replied. "You're the best shortstop in our block. What are you up to anyway?"

"Trying to find out what really happened to Mr. Sakata," I said. "You were at the movies last night. Did you see anything?"

Joey stared at his glove. After a moment, he looked up and answered.

"Nope," he said. "I was just watching the movie. Roy Rogers westerns are my favorite."

"I see," I said.

After talking to Joey, I continued on to John's barracks. He was surprised to see me.

"Tommy, what are you doing here?" John said, opening the door and pulling me inside.

"Trying to help you," I replied.

"You shouldn't be here," he said. "The head security officer doesn't want me talking to anyone until the case goes to trial."

"I just need to know a few things. Where were you when Mr. Sakata was attacked?" I asked.

"I had gone to your mess hall to see what movie was playing," he said. "It turned out to be a Gene Autry western. I stayed in the back for a while and then left. That's when I found the other guards searching my locker."

"Did you recognize anyone else at the movie?" I asked.

"Victor Kudo," John replied. "He denies seeing me there, even though I know he did. Without him, I have no proof."

"We'll see about that," I said, looking around the room.

I had my first clue, but I wasn't sure what it meant. I knew I had to question the one person I didn't want to see again.

I walked across the street to the camp's youth social club. A group of older teens were playing basketball. I spotted Victor taking a breather near the sideline.

"Could I talk to you?" I asked him.

"What do you want?" Victor said.

"You were at the movie the night Mr. Sakata was attacked," I said. "John remembers seeing you there. Yet, you told the security officer you weren't there. You lied."

"So?" said Victor. He stood up and looked me in the eyes. I could see his bully friends approaching from behind.

I didn't back down. "Well, that would prove that John didn't do it," I said.

I was now pretty sure I knew what happened and why. After I left Victor, I double-checked a few things. Once I was confident that I knew the facts, I told the security officer my theory of the crime.

CHAPTER 6

Case Closed

The security officer asked everyone involved to meet in the mess hall after breakfast.

"You all know why you are here," the security officer said. "A crime has been committed and a guard stands accused.

"However, one person, Tommy Yamamoto, was determined to prove that Private John O'Malley was innocent. I did something a little unusual. I let Tommy poke around a bit. I figured he could find things out that I couldn't.

"Or, he would get tired and drop it. So you could imagine my surprise when he came to me last night and told me his theory. And now he is going to share it with you. Go ahead, Tommy."

43

"I didn't think it could be Mr. Collins," I continued. "He had never done anything violent before.

"When I went to visit John, I noticed that his bed and locker are right next to Collins's. That got me thinking," I said, continuing to circle the room. "What if someone was out to frame Collins but framed John by mistake?

"There are a lot of people in camp that were very happy to see a soldier in trouble. Victor Kudo came to mind. John told me that he saw Victor during the movie. Even though Victor denied it at first, he finally admitted that he saw John at the movies. So, they both couldn't have done it.

"At this point, I remembered something I read in the Sherlock Holmes novel, *The Sign of the Four*. Holmes tells Dr. Watson that when you have eliminated the impossible, whatever remains must be the truth."

"I didn't do it!" Joey shouted.

"But all the pieces fit," I said. "You told me that you enjoyed the Roy Rogers movie. But that night, a Gene Autry western was shown instead. I know because I spoke with the person who ran the film that night."

"Then there is the cut above your wrist," I continued. "You said you got it playing baseball. But, the cut was already scabbed over when I saw it. I think you got the cut when you snuck up on Mr. Sakata and snatched the carving."

"It was an accident," replied Joey. "It was dark outside, and I had set my baseball bat down. Mr. Sakata tripped over it. When I saw him fall, I got scared and ran. I panicked and hid in the officer's barrack."

"Yeah, Collins let me borrow it earlier that afternoon," John said.

"What's going to happen to Joey?" I asked the head officer.

"He will be confined to quarters for ninety days," he replied. "Of course, that does not include any punishment his parents give him. Do you understand, young man?"

"Yes, sir," Joey said. "I'm sorry for all the trouble I have caused."

"As for you Tommy, you should be proud of yourself," the head officer continued. "You stood up for a friend and did the right thing despite the trouble you faced for doing it."

"Thank you, sir," I said.

As the crowd began to leave the mess hall, I spotted my mother sitting in the back row. I didn't know she had come.

I knew that some day my father would join us at camp. We would be a family again. Until then, my hero, Sherlock Holmes, would get me through the long days. Holmes helped people who were wrongly accused of crimes. At Manzanar, I learned just how important it was to stand up for innocence.

About the Author

Eric Fein is a freelance writer and editor. He has edited books for Marvel and DC Comics, which included well-known characters such as Batman, Superman, Wonder Woman, and Spider-Man. Fein has also written dozens of graphic novels and educational children's books. He currently lives in Ridgefield Park, New Jersey.

About the Illustrator

Before becoming an illustrator, Kurt Hartman had many jobs. He was a carpenter, a painter, a set dresser, an art director, a scenic artist for movies, a production designer, and much more. Today, he works as an illustrator and designer in Los Angeles, California. He lives with his wife Lauren, their children, Henry and Abigail, and far too many cats.

Glossary

agent (AY-juhnt)—an official who works for a government organization such as the FBI

barracks (BA-ruhks)—the buildings where military soldiers live

citizens (SIT-ih-zhuhz)—members of a country who have the right to live there

immigrant (IM-uh-gruhnt)—someone who has moved from one country to another country

infirmary (in-FUR-mur-ee)—a place where sick or injured people are cared for or treated

internment camp (IN-turn-muhnt CAMP)—a place used to hold suspected enemies during a war

investigation (in-VESS-tuh-gay-shuhn)—a close study of a crime to find out as much about the event as possible

quarters (KWOR-turz)—the lodging or rooms where people live, often during military combat

suspect (SUHSS-pekt)—someone thought to be responsible for committing a crime

More About the Manzanar Relocation Center

On December 7, 1941, Japanese planes attacked the U.S. Pacific Fleet on the island of Oahu, Hawaii. In less than two hours of fighting, 2,403 Americans died during the raid. One day later, December 8, 1941, President Franklin D. Roosevelt asked the U.S. Congress to declare war on Japan.

As the United States entered World War II (1939–1945), suspicion against Japanese Americans started to grow. Some people believed these citizens could really be spies working for the enemy, Japan. On February 19, 1942, President Roosevelt signed Executive Order 9066. The document allowed the U.S. military to remove potentially dangerous citizens from the West Coast.

In the following months, 120,000 Japanese Americans were forced from their homes. These innocent citizens were moved to ten different housing camps, often called internment camps or relocation centers. Many would be held there for the next four years.

Manzanar Relocation Center in the desert of California housed 11,070 Japanese Americans. As with other camps, more than half of these internees were children. Although these children still attended school, life for them was anything but normal. Their families were forced to share small rooms with other families. In some camps, residents had little food to eat and poor medical care. Temperatures in the desert could reach 110 degrees Fahrenheit (43 degrees Celsius).

Even with these challenges, life for Japanese Americans continued. While at Manzanar, 188 couples were married. Dozens of students received their college degrees. Some residents even served in the military, fighting for the United States in World War II.

Soon after the war ended, Manzanar Relocation Center closed on August 14, 1945. In 1992, the camp became a National Historic Site. Today, visitors can learn about the unfair treatment of these American citizens, and how they succeeded despite the obstacles.

Discussion Questions

1. During World War II (1939–1945), the United
   States government sent many Japanese
   Americans to relocation centers like Manzanar.
   The government believed they could be spies for
   Japan. How do you feel about this decision? Do
   you think it was wrong for the U.S. government
   to suspect all Japanese Americans of spying?
   Why or why not?

2. In the story, some of the guards at Manzanar
   treated people poorly. So why do you think
   Tommy wanted to help one of the guards?
   Would you have done the same?

3. In the end, Tommy's friend Joey turned out to be
   the thief. Do you think Tommy should have told
   on his best friend? If your friend committed a
   crime, would you tell on them?

Writing Prompts

1. This story is known as historical fiction. The historical event is true, but the characters are fictional. Choose your favorite historical event. Then make up a story that happens on that day.

2. At the end of the book, Tommy believes he will be reunited with his father soon. What do you think? Write a story about what happens next.

3. Write your own mystery. Who will solve the case? Who will be the suspects? And who will be the real criminal? It's up to you!

Internet Sites

Do you want to know more about subjects related to this book? Or are you interested in learning about other topics? Then check out FactHound, a fun, easy way to find Internet sites.

Our investigative staff has already sniffed out great sites for you!

Here's how to use FactHound:

1. Visit *www.facthound.com*

2. Select your grade level.

3. To learn more about subjects related to this book, type in the book's ISBN number: 9781434207517.

4. Click the **Fetch It** button.

FactHound will fetch the best Internet sites for you.